THE STORY OF
NOICHI
THE BLIND

CHET WILLIAMSON

Introduction

By Chet Williamson

That the following work of fiction survives at all is nearly as unlikely as the events that occur in and around the hut of Noichi the woodcutter in the tale itself. My son Colin, a resident of Japan for the past seven years, must take credit for discovering the manuscript in a serendipitous turn of events.

One afternoon he was waiting for a friend in Ueno, a district of Tokyo, when he decided to kill some time by going into a rather shabby antique shop. One of Colin's hobbies is photography, and, although he uses mostly high-end digital equipment, he has a fascination for older cameras as well, and often tinkers with old analog cameras and parts. When he inquired after such items, the owner of the shop told him that there was a box of old and mostly broken cameras in the storage area that he could examine.

Though Colin found nothing of interest in the box, next to it was another small box full of a mix of Japanese and English language books, a few of them surprisingly pre-war. The item that caught his eye was a *manga* that dated to the 1950s. It was in Japanese, but also stated "A Ghost Story" in English on the cover. The condition was rough, but it was the type of piece he knew I would like.

The owner said that he had bought the box as part of an estate, and that, since he didn't really sell books, he would prefer to sell the whole box rather than just the individual *manga*. He offered Colin the box for three thousand yen. Since Colin suspected that the *manga* alone was worth that price, he agreed and handed over the equivalent of thirty dollars.

That night when he got home he went through the rest of the contents and found little of interest except for a few pre-war volumes on Japanese natural history, which he decided to take to an actual used book dealer. The bottom of the box was padded with old, yellowed newspapers, and when he took them out to toss into the proper recycling bin he found a torn and stained manila envelope, inside of which was the following manuscript. It was as badly stained as the envelope that held it and bore the faint but unmistakable pungency of cat urine. Still, he read it, and upon doing so he decided to send it to me.

To pique my interest he scanned and emailed me the first page. I have to confess that it failed to excite me, seeming to be a very flat retelling of some Japanese folk tale. Colin assured me, however, that the tone changed dramatically, and when the manuscript arrived by airmail a week later (along with the *manga*, which I was looking forward to far more than the manuscript), I found that he was right. The story was a quite disturbing one, written somewhat in the style of Lafcadio Hearn.

Hearn, for those not familiar with him, was the son of an Irish father and a Greek mother, and his first name was a variant of the name of the Greek island on which he was born in 1850. He came to America in 1869, where he began his writing career as a reporter for Cincinnati and New Orleans newspapers, writing mostly about dark and violent events. After travels in the West Indies, he went to Japan in 1890, where he remained until his death in 1904. He married a Japanese wife, became a naturalized citizen of Japan, and took the name of Yakumo Koizumi. Hearn has become known as one of the first (and finest) writers to interpret and explain Japanese culture to the West, and retold many classic Japanese ghost stories and horror tales, his best-known collection of these being *Kwaidan*, published in the year of his death.

It took me some time to discover Hearn's work, for the paperback horror anthologists I read while growing up seldom used his stories, with a few exceptions: I read "Jikininki" in Bernhardt J. Hurwood's 1965 *Monsters Galore*, and Basil Davenport reprinted the short-short, "Mujina," in the 1953 *Tales to Be Told in the Dark*, which I read in the later paperback edition. The story inspired a very unpleasant nightmare in which a blank, egg-shaped head drifted up from behind the headboard of my bed. At last I found and was haunted by *Kwaidan*, and with my son's own spiritual and physical expatriation to Japan, my interest in Hearn and in all things Japanese has continued to grow.

It's obvious that "The Story of Noichi the Blind" possesses some parallels to Hearn's work (for a detailed discussion, see the afterword to this volume, graciously written by Dr. Alan Drew of the University of Western Michigan). Still, I couldn't begin to imagine, nor can I now, that it could possibly be a previously unknown work by Hearn. But if I wished to learn who the true author was, it certainly made sense to rule out Hearn as quickly as possible.

My first move was to key several phrases from the story into various search engines to determine if the story was in print online, but there were no matches. I then went through the writings of Hearn himself, many of which I found online. One of the local college libraries boasts the 16-volume Koizumi Edition of Hearn's collected works, published in 1922, and I searched through these as well, but the story was not to be found.

Now that I knew the story was not a previously known Hearn work, I decided to investigate further by trying to somehow date the manuscript itself. I know nothing about typefaces, but I could see that the paper was *washi*, the traditional Japanese paper made from plant fibers. It's strong and light and very durable, and though I wouldn't have thought it would make good typing paper, it seemed to have aged well, despite the stains and the unpleasant smell, of which one received only a hint when holding it at arm's length.

I made a photocopy of the complete manuscript, then contacted Richard Polt, whom I had met through our mutual interest in mystery writer Harry Stephen Keeler (Richard runs the website for the Keeler Society at: site.xavier.edu/polt/keeler). Another hobby of his is old and antique typewriters (site.xavier.edu/polt/typewriters), and when I sent him a query he offered to examine one of the typewritten sheets to try and determine its vintage. I was reluctant to entrust even a single sheet to the mails, but Richard received it safely.

He replied that the evenness of the impressions suggested to him that it could have been typed on one of the Hammond typewriters, which were quite popular in the late 1800s and early 1900s, and were sold in many countries. On this machine, unlike others, each keystroke tripped a hammer that struck the paper from behind, forcing it against the ribbon and the type instead of *vice versa*, so that the typeface produced the same amount of force with each stroke, no matter how hard or lightly one hit the individual key. A later email from him told me that a friend of his who is an expert on typescripts definitely identified the typeface as from a Hammond type shuttle.

Of course, all this proved only that the manuscript was typed on a vintage machine and possibly on vintage paper, but it could have been typed as early as the 1890s or as late as the 1990s, if someone had had access to such a classic machine. On the other hand, there is no logic to someone creating a vintage literary hoax only to have a cat urinate on it and then put it at the bottom of a three-thousand-yen bargain box in the back room of a shabby Ueno shop, so I thought it safe to assume that at least its age was authentic.

When I let my imagination wander unhindered, the best-case scenario was that this could indeed be an original story (or a retelling of an earlier Japanese folk tale) by Lafcadio Hearn. A more rational explanation, however, was that it was probably written by an English-language author living in Japan who was greatly influenced by him. This latter possibility was far easier to imagine, for Hearn's popularity in the United States and Europe after his death was at its highest, and it's not far-fetched to picture a young American or British writer, filled to the mental brim with Hearn's dark tales of oriental *liebestod*, coming to the country that was the source of his inspiration and attempting to follow in his literary mentor's footsteps.

However, in terms of sexual explicitness and graphic violence, "The Story of Noichi the Blind" goes beyond anything that Hearn ever wrote, at least for publication, though I fear it does not come close to equaling even his lesser efforts artistically. That the story was not publishable — or even palatable — in the first part of the twentieth century should come as no surprise, since it's unpleasantly strong fare even in today's environment of extreme fiction. If it ever *was* published, it was surely by some small press that printed their works by the dozens, for sale by subscription only to a very specialized clientele.

But all this is speculation, speculation that receives a far more practical and earthbound perspective in the afterword by Dr. Drew, to whom I sent a copy of the manuscript shortly after I confirmed its age. A lifelong Hearn scholar, he is the author of *Lafcadio Hearn: A Spark in the Shadows*, and it was primarily through his efforts that a publisher was secured for the present volume. Dr. Drew's essay following the story itself will shine more light on the question of authorship for the curious reader.

"The Story of Noichi the Blind" is offered here as, to paraphrase Hearn's own words modestly describing his stories in *Kottō*, a Japanese curio, with sundry cobwebs. I might caution those with more delicate tastes to go no further, for this is not the Japan of white *sakura* drifting like snow from the cherry trees in springtime, but a far more dark and cruel country inhabited by the innocent, the foolish, and the monsters that prey upon them. Still, since my own literary tastes swing toward the *contes cruel*, I found it a Japan worth visiting, one long gone and perhaps better so.

As Hearn himself said of his adopted country, in words that ironically reflect the soul of this tale's title character, "What is there, finally, to love in Japan except what is passing away?"

Editorial Note

We have tried to keep any editorial intrusion to a minimum. Our intent has been to reproduce as closely as possible the original typescript, including all idiosyncrasies of punctuation and formatting. Some paragraphs may seem quite long, particularly in light of current practice, but we have resisted the urge to break these lengthy paragraphs into shorter ones. Underlined dialogue in the typescript has been consistently treated as italics. Though several typographical errors in spelling and punctuation (primarily commas for periods and *vice versa*) have been corrected, no other changes have been made.

The Story of
Noichi the Blind

In the province of Harima, a woodcutter and his wife lived high in the hills. The woodcutter's name was Noichi, and all week long he would fell trees from the great stands of pine and bamboo that made up the vast forest. Then he and his wife Noriko hewed them into sticks small enough to fit into stoves. At the end of the week they stacked the wood onto a small flat cart to which Noichi hitched the horse. Then Noriko would pile another stack of light branches onto Noichi's back, attaching them with woven bamboo strips, and Noichi would lead the horse down the mountain and to the nearby town of U—. There he sold the wood, and with the money he made he bought rice and other food that he and Noriko could not grow in their garden, as well as a sack of grain for the horse. On occasion Noichi bought pieces of cloth with which Noriko could mend their clothing when it grew worn.

Noichi had given the horse no name, for he did not think it fitting for a man to name another creature. He also thought that the horse might have a name of his own, known only to itself and to other horses, given to him by the gods at his birth, or when some event occurred in his life that dictated the name by which he should henceforth think of himself.

Noichi did not even address him as *horse*. He called him *my friend*, for that was how he thought of the horse.

Noichi and Noriko could not have lived without the horse, for the woodcutter and his wife working together could have carried only a small portion of the wood the horse bore. The horse's strength and willingness to serve made their existence possible, and Noichi was grateful.

Noichi's solicitousness extended to all the creatures of the wood, and had ever since he came alone into the forest. His first intention had been to become a priest, but he had found that his fellow novitiates and even most of the priests were obsessed with the Self, and he left the temple only a short time after his arrival.

He wished to live alone in the woods, so he worked shoveling dung until he had amassed enough money to buy an axe, and then went up into the hills. There he built a simple hut to keep him from the rain and cold, and he began to cut wood. But Noichi quickly learned that he could not carry enough wood to the town of U—to sustain himself. The woods were abundant with animals, but the thought never passed his mind of killing any for meat. That he simply would not do.

One day while Noichi was working in a stand of bamboo he heard an unfamiliar sound break the forest's silence. He turned and saw a horse walking slowly through the trees, carrying a rider on its back. At first, Noichi thought that it might be a ghost, for although the rider's eyes were open wide, his face was white, and a great wound had opened his belly, so that loops of red entrails hung down on either side of the horse's flanks.

Noichi watched the specter (for such he thought it) approach, but when he saw that the rider neither moved nor spoke, and saw that the horse's body was wet with flecks of sweat, and that its mouth dripped bubbles of white foam, he surmised the truth. The warrior was dead, his horse exhausted.

For the man was a warrior. Though he held no katana in his hand, an empty sheath hung at his side and he bore the trappings of a samurai. There was no family crest, so Noichi felt certain he was a masterless ronin. The young woodcutter easily guessed the rest. There had been a confrontation of some sort, the warrior had been slain, his sword fallen from his dead or dying hand, and his horse had fled from the scene of combat, possibly in the hopes of preserving its master's life, possibly through blind instinct.

The ronin, however, had not fallen from his mount, even in death. Noichi saw that his feet were wedged firmly in the stirrups, and that his toes were pointed outward, so that the sharp spurs remained pressed against the horse's flank. Pity filled the woodcutter's soul as he looked at the weary horse, driven onward by a dead rider who would not be content until his partner in battle joined him in death. Even now, driven beyond endurance, the horse plodded on, weaving aimlessly between the bamboo trees.

Making soothing sounds, Noichi approached the right side of the caparisoned beast, which nickered weakly but still moved onward. He fell into step beside it, touching its great neck with his calloused hand, trying to soothe it.

Then he grasped the warrior's right foot, pulled it outward so that the spur no longer pressed its sharp barb against the horse's flesh, and yanked it out of the stirrup. The horse immediately swung toward Noichi, its great shoulder knocking him to the forest floor and sending him scrambling to avoid being trod upon by the iron shod hooves.

The samurai's body tipped to the left and fell. When it did, the left spur also disengaged from the horse's side and, free at last of its sharp goad, the animal stopped, its legs straddling the supine Noichi. The dead man's left foot slipped from the stirrup, and the corpse fell next to Noichi. Its entrails followed, sliding off the horse's back directly onto Noichi's face. The woodcutter gasped as the cold wetness coiled about him, and the horror made him push himself to his feet, heedless of the horse's powerful hooves. But the beast moved not at all. It merely stood exhausted, its flanks moving fitfully with its ragged breathing. The fresh blood oozing from the wounds where the spurs had gouged the horse was like bright coral to the dark rust of the ronin's dried blood that coated its back.

Noichi stood and patted the animal's drooping neck, then gave it water from a wooden bowl that he had brought to assuage his thirst as he cut the trees. The horse quickly drank it all, and Noichi ran to the spring to get more. The horse was there when he returned, and consumed what was newly offered. Then Noichi carefully removed the saddle and bridle from the beast, which sank down upon the soft and matted ground, closed its eyes, and went to sleep upon the instant.

From the forest, Noichi gathered an assortment of leaves and roots that he ground between stones into poultices, and rubbed them gently into the spur wound on the left side of the sleeping horse, which snorted softly but did not wake. While it continued to sleep, Noichi returned to his hut and brought the horse a large bowl of grain, as well as more water from the spring.

When the horse awoke, it ate and drank, and allowed Noichi to apply the salve to its right side as well. With a flat rock Noichi dug a grave and buried the samurai and all his accoutrements. Attempting to sell them in U—might have raised too many questions. The saddle and bridle he hid in the woods.

For two days the horse regained its strength, while Noichi brought it grain and water and tended to its wounds. At last, when he went back to his hut, it followed him. Over the next few weeks, Noichi built a cart out of some of the wood he had felled, and constructed from the leather of the saddle and bridle a harness with which he could yoke the horse to the cart. He was hesitant to attempt this at first, but was pleased to find that the horse readily accepted both the harness and the job. Noichi was thus able to carry far more wood into the town of U—, and his income greatly increased.

Noichi and the horse, for he never thought of it as *his* horse, lived in mutual respect and cooperation. It took a full day to go into the town of U—and return to the forest, but on the way back Noichi never rode in the cart, which carried only their supplies. He walked beside the horse, carrying provisions as well, for he felt the burden should be shared. When they arrived home, Noichi never hitched or otherwise tried to restrain the horse. It roamed free, and if it decided to leave him, that was its right, though it never did.

Noichi's treatment of the horse as an equal did not go unnoticed by the other creatures that lived in the forest. The birds and animals, from the snakes that crept on their bellies to the hawks that inhabited the highest trees, were all aware of Noichi's gentleness and kindness. If a bird had a nest in a tree, Noichi would not cut it down. If the den of a weasel or a rabbit was buried in the shelter of the roots, he spared that tree as well. When he fetched water from the spring and walked by the stream into which it fed, he trod carefully to avoid stepping on a crayfish or a lizard or a frog at the water's edge. Even when he felled a tree, he would first determine that its fall would harm no living thing.

Noichi's natural domain became a haven for the animals and birds, and in time even those who preyed upon others, like the hawks and the wildcats, foraged elsewhere, as though shamed by Noichi's behavior. Though attacking and feeding on other creatures was in their very nature, they seemed to sense that this part of the forest was not a place in which such things should be done, and so took their slaughter elsewhere.

The animals would come to Noichi's fire on cold nights, sitting so close to him that he could reach out and touch them, and when any were harmed they came to him and he used his salves and poultices to heal them if he could. The birds would fly about him as he did his work, singing their songs for him, and sit on his shoulders when he paused to rest. Noichi would talk to them and whistle their songs back to them, and they would fly up circling with delight.

In Noichi's twenty-fifth year, he found Noriko. She was a servant in the house of a woman who kept courtesans in the poorest section of the town of U—. Though young, Noriko was not comely, and had been sold at the age of thirteen by her parents, farmers to whom the immediate profit was of greater import than any work Noriko might do for them. She had been a sickly child, and the medicines bought to keep her alive were of far greater expense than the value of her potential service. The procurer had wagered on the possibility that a life of indoor servitude might prove less taxing than the strenuous outdoor life, and so it proved to be.

Though Noriko did not thrive, neither did she sicken within the brothel's walls. She remained preternaturally thin, due as much to her limited diet of rice as to her constitutional weakness. Fish or meat or vegetables seldom if ever passed through her lips, and her boniness and the unattractiveness of her features (she had a long nose and a prognathous jaw) were enough to secure her from the molestations of the clientele and assure that she retained her virtue.

One night, however, a band of eight samurai visited the brothel. On that particular night, only seven of the procurer's nine women were available. The remaining two were in the strongest time of their monthly flow, and the youngest samurai, who was the last to make his selection, wanted naught to do with either of them.

Then the captain of the samurai, an older man with numerous grey hairs amid the black, told the youngest warrior to take the girl that he himself had chosen, the most attractive of the lot. When asked by his followers how he would slake his own hunger, he grunted toward Noriko, who sat, so she had thought, unnoticed in a dark corner.

The girl is a servant, said the procurer. *Not a courtesan.*

I like the set of that jaw, the captain said, then smiled a thin smile. *I can do things with that jaw.*

The captain spilled a handful of coins onto the worn tatami, and the procurer crept over to Noriko, who had heard every word and had begun to tremble. *Go with him and do as he says, or I shall beat you harder than I ever have before. I may even kill you and throw your body into the sewer pit if you do not heed.*

So Noriko, though filled with fear, went with the old captain into a room. There he made her undress until not a piece of her clothing remained, and then he removed his own garments. His tool was small, but stuck up straight and hard, and he first bade her play upon it like a flute, instructing her how she should use her lips and tongue. Then he positioned her on her elbows and knees, wrapped the hilt of his tanto in a strip of silk, rubbed grease upon it, and put it inside her womb, while he forced his own tool into her nether eye just above. Noriko had never known such pain. There was not a trace of the pleasure of which the courtesans had boasted. She bit her lip to try and keep from shouting out, but she could not help it, and her cries seemed to further ignite the captain so that he pressed both tool and knife hilt more savagely into her.

At last she could bear no more, and scampered forward, away from him, so that his tool was wrenched out of her backside. The hilt of the tanto, however, remained tightly wedged so that Noriko's forward movement freed it from its sheath, and the naked, razor sharp blade now protruded from within her.

The captain, enraged by what he saw as the mutiny of a whore, and not realizing in his heat that he now held an empty sheath, lunged forward to retrieve his fleshy vessel, and in doing so he succeeded only in impaling himself upon his own tanto. His surprised groan of pain sang along with Noriko's squeal of agony as the hilt battered the walls of her womb, making her jerk forward again, pulling the blade out of the captain's belly while also slicing it open.

Gasping, Noriko reached between her legs and cut her fingers on the protruding knife. Then she made herself delve more carefully, gripped the stub of the hilt near the blade, and withdrew it from her with a sensation of both pain and relief. Then she looked at the captain. He was on his knees, his knuckles on the mat supporting his upper body. Blood was running from his opened bowels, and he looked, Noriko thought, like a cow giving red milk. His expression, however, was not that of placid docility that she had seen on the cow on her father's farm, but rather one of utter surprise and disbelief, as though the captain was thinking that surely he could not have been slain by a knife in a whore's hole. Then the look of surprise was replaced by no look whatsoever. The knuckles turned under, the wrists buckled, and the captain fell dead.

For a long time Noriko lay there, propped on one elbow, her other hand between her legs to comfort her pain. She knew that if she did not flee she would be killed by the other samurai, even though the captain's death was not her fault. She listened to the sounds about her, hearing nothing but the grunting of the samurai and their courtesans, and knowing that the sounds she and the captain had made, no matter how violent, had blended into them. The others would be at it for a while longer. If she were to go, it must be now.

She ripped some strips off her undergarments, folded them into pads, and used them to staunch the blood that dripped from her. Then she got dressed. Owning nothing, there was nothing to take, and she slipped out of the brothel and let the night engulf her.

Noriko walked out of U—until the north road turned eastward. She stepped off of it, and kept going north into the hills. She walked through the woods until she came upon a partly overgrown road with parallel ruts, and followed that higher into the hills. She had no idea where she was headed, but felt certain that the samurai would seek her on the southern road that led to the larger towns.

By midday Noriko was weary with her travels. Her bleeding had stopped, although the soreness was exacerbated with every step she took. Still, she pressed on, walking in the ruts of the road, the grasses high around her, and off the road the trees higher still. She was moving slower, dragging her feet with every step, until at last her legs would no longer bear her, and she fell to her knees, crawled off the road into the deep grass, and fell asleep.

Noriko?

When she opened her eyes it seemed as if she had slept for only an moment. A man looked down at her, and he looked familiar, and she knew he must be one of the captain's samurai she had seen the night before, and she prepared herself for death.

I am Noichi, the man said, and she saw that he was not dressed as a samurai and bore no sword. *Noichi the woodcutter.* And then she knew him as the man from whom the procurer bought firewood every week.

Noichi gave her water from a flask and bade her eat a rice ball. He told her that he was returning from his weekly trip to U—and that the town was filled with the news that she had killed a samurai captain, and that she was being sought on both the south and the northeast roads.

It isn't true, she said, and Noichi said that she could tell him about it later if she cared to. He helped her to the horse cart, bade her lay in the back, and made her as comfortable as he could. Then they continued north. Though she tried to stay awake, she could not.

Noriko awoke when the motion of the cart stopped. It was nearly dark, and Noichi helped her to her feet and led her into a small hut made of logs, where he invited her to lie upon a sleeping mat. He gave her more rice and a few vegetables, then covered her with a thin blanket and told her to sleep.

She did not wake until midmorning, when Noichi gave her some tea and rice. Then she told him everything that had happened to her with the captain. She left nothing out, but Noichi was so frank and kind that she felt little embarrassment. His expression showed deep sympathy, and suggested that he knew that none of this had been her choice, that she had had such misfortune and misery visited upon her against her will.

When her story was told, Noichi said that she was welcome to remain with him for as long as she liked, that no one ever visited him, and that no samurai would ever look for her there. She could care for his hut and cook the rice and tend the vegetables in the garden while Noichi cut his wood.

And so they lived together for a time, learning more about each other, and caring more every day, one for the other, until one day in the fall Noichi asked Noriko if she would be his wife, and she agreed. Since they could be bound by no priest, any one of whom might be aware of Noriko's status as a fugitive, they took their vows under the open sky before the gods, promising each to cleave to the other and remain faithful unto death — and even after death, Noichi added, and Noriko agreed.

But for the occasional touch of a hand or a fraternal pat of the shoulder, they had never been physically close to one another. That evening Noriko put her sleeping mat next to Noichi's and lay down. Noichi lay down as well, but made no attempt to embrace Noriko, fearful that such intimacy might quickly bring to his wife's mind the terrible evening with the captain of samurai.

They lay for a time, until Noriko said, *Should we do what it is fitting that a husband and wife should do?*

Only if it is your wish, Noichi answered.

I think it is my wish, said Noriko, *unless you find me…unless you do not wish to.*

It is my wish if it is yours.

Noichi embraced her then, but delicately, as one holds a thin vase of fine glass in fear of breaking it. Noriko returned his embrace, tentatively as well, then with more ardor, and in a time they were engaging fully in the acts of a man and a maid. When they had coupled, however, Noichi sensed that his wife was feeling discomfort, and he ceased his motions. Noriko urged him on, but the dryness of her passage brought him discomfort as well, and he stopped once more.

Noriko began to weep, not from the pain but rather disappointment in her inability to satisfy her new husband. He comforted her, telling her that all would be well, and the next day when his work was done, he gathered certain leaves and roots and ground them into a salve with which he told Noriko to cleanse herself before they once again conjoined. She did so, and the results were felicitous. Indeed, their couplings grew to be pleasant and greatly looked forward to by both.

Were they to pleasure each other by day, the birds would perch on the window openings and sing their songs for Noriko and Noichi, and the rabbits and squirrels would sit in the doorway, heads cocked in contemplation. After dark the creatures of the night served as the attendees to their human friends, the weasels and the frogs and the bats and the serpents who had slept all day in the sun, reveling in the joy of the couple, and in the natural and free expression of love that was the birthright and the means of perpetuation of all creatures.

Perpetuation, however, did not come for Noichi and Noriko. Her womb was barren, whether from the brutalities visited upon her by the samurai captain or from other causes they did not know. Her inability to bear a child was the only shadow in their lives together. As Noichi had promised, no one ever came to the hut in search of the fugitive Noriko, nor for any other reason whatever.

Life went on, and every week Noichi and the horse descended into the town of U—with the firewood, and returned with rice and grain and whatever else they would need in the week to come. Noriko became as good a friend to the creatures of the forest as Noichi, and what had begun as merely a lack of fear on the part of the birds and animals grew into affection and devotion.

They lived in this manner for several years, until Noriko became ill. Noichi had noticed her pallor, and had insisted that she try and eat more, giving up much of his own rice to her. She could not keep the food in her stomach, however, and soon Noichi saw that what she had vomited up contained blood, as well as shreds of flesh from deep inside her. Noichi tried to control his fears, and gathered roots and plants in order to restore Noriko to health, but nothing that he gave her did any good.

Noichi decided to seek the help of a physician, but realized that anyone in the town of U—might remember Noriko's involvement in the death of the captain, so he took the northeast road to the town of H—. It was a walk of a day and a half, and Noichi arrived in the evening. No one knew him and he knew no one in H—, but he found a physician by the marker on the man's house. Noichi told him that his wife was very ill, and begged him to come with him, but the doctor looked at Noichi's poor clothing and demanded money first. Noichi gave him the few coins he had left from his earnings the previous week, and told the doctor he had more at his home. Noichi had never before told a lie, but he felt as though he would have done anything to make Noriko well again.

Noichi had not told the physician how far his hut was, and when dawn rose the next day the man was angry that they were not yet there, and told Noichi that the visit would cost far more than he had originally stated. Noichi said that was of no matter, and that he would pay the doctor whatever he wished, but from the disdainful way the man continued to look at Noichi and his shabby clothing he knew the physician doubted him.

They walked on, and finally the physician took the wooden box of medicines from his girdle and brusquely ordered Noichi to carry it. It was heavy, and Noichi was surprised that the man had been able to bear it so long without complaint.

By the time they turned off the road to the northeast and onto Noichi's cart-trail, the physician was furious, and demanded that if Noichi could not pay his fee, he would have to bring the physician firewood every week until the fee was finally paid off. Noichi had every intention of doing so, and told the doctor that, but still was not believed.

By mid-afternoon they arrived at the hut, and Noichi ran inside to see how Noriko had fared during the three days he had had to leave her alone. The birds that had been hovering about her and the rabbits and squirrels that had been keeping watch initially fled at his abrupt approach before they realized that it was the gentle Noichi who had always been so kind to them. They stopped just as Noichi reached the side of his wife and looked at her.

Noriko was lying right where he had left her. She looked even more pale and thin than before. The rice balls that he had left for her to eat were still where he had placed them, all except for one. The remains of that one lay on the earth floor, the white grains mixed with the blood from when Noriko's stomach had refused to hold it down. The level of water in the large bowl Noichi had left for her was down only by the thickness of two fingers.

Noriko looked more dead than alive. The fullness of her countenance had tautened so that the flesh of her cheeks had fallen in, and her pronounced nose jutted even more sharply from her face, a sickle moon rising between the jagged mountains of her cheekbones. Dried blood sat like a raw birthmark on her chin, and Noichi dipped the hem of his garment into the water bowl and tenderly wiped it away.

Noriko's eyes opened. The whites had gone yellow, and Noichi sensed that Noriko did not see him. He told her that it was he, and that he had brought a doctor who would make her well again. She nodded her head just a bit and closed her eyes again. The physician came up behind Noichi and looked at Noriko is a businesslike sort of way.

You can make her well again, can't you? Noichi asked him, but the longer the man looked at Noriko the more his face soured.

Then the physician's eyes grew wide and he said, *This is the woman who killed Captain Okeda.*

Noichi said nothing. He only looked at the man as though he had no understanding of what he had said.

The whore, the doctor went on. *You are hiding her. The samurai told us what she looked like. This is her, isn't it?*

Can you make her well? Noichi asked. *I will give you all I have, I will pledge my life to you, be your servant until I die.*

You have nothing. I thought as much back in H—, but I was fool enough to trust you. And what good is the pledge of a poor woodcutter? You can do nothing for me.

Noichi knew that all this was true, and that he had dishonored himself by his lies. Still, he could not let Noriko die, now that a doctor was here. *You must save her,* he said. *You are here, you have your medicines, your skills. Please save her.*

Save her? the physician scoffed. *How can I save her? She is nearly dead. And as well she should be. The gods have judged her for her crime, and I will let the authorities know that she was here and how she died, and that you sheltered her, and then they shall come and take you, and so you too shall die.*

Noichi could not believe his ill fortune. Still, he could not let Noriko die. *Do with me what you will. Kill me now if you like*—and he gestured to the doctor's sword—*only save her.*

Save a murderess? I cannot. And I would not if I could.

Noichi thought for a moment, then knelt by the doctor's heavy box of medicines and started to open it.

Fool! the doctor cried, and he drew his sword, raising it for an overhand stroke to split Noichi's spine. But the birds flew about the physician's head, their wings slapping at his cheeks and their sharp little beaks pecking at his face, stabbing into the softness of his eyes and blinding him. The weasels leapt upon his arms, tearing at his hands and wrists with their sharp teeth and claws so that his sword fell from his hand. The snakes sank their fangs into his legs, pumping their poison into him. Even the rabbits sprang into the air on their strong legs and nipped at his throat, tearing away small bits of flesh while the squirrels scampered up and over his clothing, their sharp chisel teeth scraping through cloth and skin.

The physician, blinded and bloodied from dozens of small yet agonizing wounds, thrashed about madly until he staggered through the doorway of the hut. His arms flailed as he tried to batter the creatures that were attacking him. But for every one he threw off, two more took its place. At last, poisoned and weak from loss of blood, he fell to the earth, and his body vanished beneath a blanket of roiling fur, feathers, and scales.

Noichi had followed the creatures outside, shouting to them to leave the doctor alone, but his pleas went unheeded, and as the birds and snakes and animals withdrew one by one from their prey, there was revealed to Noichi's horrified eyes a mass of torn flesh and cloth red with gore. The doctor's face was unrecognizable, swollen with poison, the eyes dark wet hollows, the mouth a yawning cave of black blood.

What shall I do? Noichi thought, and with shame he realized that his present concern was how to hide the doctor's corpse rather than how to save Noriko's life. His dear wife must come first. So he closed his eyes on the body, then turned and went into the hut, where he opened the box of medicine, studied the writing on the labels of the many bottles and vials inside, and tried to decide which he should give to Noriko.

While Noichi worked, the creatures at the spring had become aware of what had transpired at the hut, and the news ran along the stream into which the spring fed. From the stream poured dozens, then hundreds, then thousands of crayfish and crabs, who scuttled up the bank on their many legs, moving like a hard clattering ocean to where the torn body of the physician lay. There they severed bits of the still warm meat with their claws and devoured flesh, muscle, ligament; heart, bowels, brain. The birds flew down, and the ravens feasted as the wrens and finches tugged the hair from the scalp and unraveled the blood-sodden clothing thread by thread, flying away with the scraps to use in building nests, and then simply flying far and wide to drop the pieces among the trees, so that the physician's hair and clothes vanished as completely as did his very flesh.

By nightfall all that remained was the man's bones, picked clean and white. The tissues joining them had been eaten as well, so that not one remained linked to another. The otters dragged the bones one by one to the stream, then dove with them to the deepest spots and left them there in rocky crevices to be worn away by the flowing waters. At last only the skull remained, and the horse reared over it and shattered it with its hooves, coming down again and again until all that remained was the dust of the broken bones and teeth, which the wings of the birds swept away.

Inside the hut, Noichi had been attempting to cure Noriko with the physician's medicines, but nothing he tried to give her would remain in her stomach. He tried medicine after medicine, but to no avail. Noriko barely even had the strength to speak, but at last she summoned up all her energies and said, *Let me die.*

No, Noichi said, putting a soothing hand upon her forehead. *You will not die. You cannot. You will live, and we will stay here and be happy. You will see, you will get better. Lie here and rest for as long as you need to in order to get back your strength, but you will. You will get better.*

But Noriko said, *I want to get well, but I cannot. I do not know how.* She was quiet for a moment, then said, *We said we would cleave to one another, even after death, but that cannot be. Hold my memory, but let me go.*

Never, said Noichi. *I have sworn before the gods.*

Noriko tried to reply, but she had no strength left. She closed her eyes and breathed heavily, as if the words she had spoken had cost her greatly.

Noichi sat by her side and held her hand, then went out to get fresh water from the spring. Not until then did he think about the body of the physician, and when he saw that it was no longer where it had been, he looked about wildly, thinking that either it had walked away on its own, or that samurai had come and found it. But, he reasoned, if the former, would the vengeful corpse not seek out the man responsible for its death? And if the latter, surely the samurai would have entered the hut to find the physician's murderer.

Then he realized that his friends who had saved him from the stroke of the man's sword by slaying him who wielded it had also disposed of the corpse. All that remained of the physician was his sword and his box of medicines, both of which Noichi could bury in the forest after he had found a cure for Noriko.

Noichi fetched a bowl of water from the spring and went back into the hut. Noriko was not breathing as fitfully as before. Her breath was lighter, and Noichi wondered if one of the medicines he had given her was working after all, if it had remained in her mouth or in her stomach long enough to do its work. He lay down beside her and looked at the gleaming eyes of the small animals sitting in the dark corners watching. Their presence calmed and reassured him. They were his friends and Noriko's friends too. He reached out for her hand and held it, and found that it was cooler than it had been. Perhaps her fever had broken as well. That had to be it. She was getting better. All she needed now was to rest. She didn't have to eat if she didn't want to. Noichi could do all the gardening and fetch the water and tend to the hut as well as cut the wood. He could do whatever he had to until Noriko got better. And even if she remained sickly and weak, that was all right too, just as long as she stayed with him.

He told her all these things, and although she did not reply he knew that she understood and that she was happy. Interlacing her cool fingers with his, he lay down next to her, closed his eyes and went to sleep.

Noichi awoke in daylight, and knew immediately that everything had changed. Noriko's hand was very cool now, and he knew she was much stronger, for when he tried to disengage his hand from her own, she clung to him with a powerful grip. Try as he might, he could not bend her fingers back for fear of breaking them, but eventually he was able to slide his fingers out of her strong, cold ones.

Noichi felt her forehead, and that was cold too, and he told Noriko that he had been right after all, that she was so much better this morning, that her fever had broken, and that she was much stronger. Then he got up and made a fire, and tried to give Noriko a drink of water, but the water only dribbled between her slightly parted lips and ran out again, over her cheeks and onto the bedding. Noichi said that it was fine if she wasn't thirsty, that she could drink and eat whenever she decided that she was ready.

Then he told her that he wanted to wash her bedding and her clothes, and that she would feel even better when she was clean once again. Noichi undressed her and in doing so found that she had soiled herself. He washed her, then removed the cloth from beneath her and covered her with a warm blanket, all the while cooing affectionate words.

Outside he made a fire and hung a pot over it and washed the clothes and bedding in the boiling water, then hung them on branches. In the cool breeze the clothing dried quickly, and by mid-afternoon Noichi had placed the bedding back on the mat and dressed Noriko once again in her simple shift. He spoke to her of the weather and of how the animals and birds had helped to dispose of the physician.

It is not right that they should have taken his life, he told Noriko, *since it was his medicines that brought you back to health. Still, they are only beasts, and they tried to aid us in the best way they knew.*

Noriko did not reply, and Noichi decided to let her rest while he went and cut more wood. He knew that he would need money to buy food to restore Noriko to full health, so he worked with vigor, and when he returned at evening Noriko was still resting, so Noichi made rice and tea.

Noriko was still not hungry, it seemed, for she did not open her mouth to accept the rice that Noichi proffered on the hachi. *Come now,* he said, *you must eat to grow stronger, yes?* He even playfully tried to open her mouth with his fingers, but her jaw stayed firmly locked in place. *You are a stubborn woman, but I can wait. You let me know when you are ready to eat, and I will have good food ready for you.*

Night had fallen, so Noichi took off his garments and lay under the blanket beside Noriko, put his arm around her, marveled again at how wonderfully cool she seemed, and went to sleep. From the dark corners and the sills of the window openings, the creatures watched their friend Noichi and wondered how to help him further.

In the morning Noichi awoke and caressed Noriko, and covered her cheeks and lips with his kisses. *Now are you hungry, my dear wife?* he asked her. *Will you eat and make your husband glad?* But when Noichi tried to feed Noriko, her mouth remained shut. Noichi kissed it and slipped his tongue between her lips, trying to make her open her mouth to accept it as she had in the past, but she did not.

You will accept neither food nor love? Then I will go and work, and hope that you will be hungry for both my rice and my kisses when I return.

Noichi ate and drank some water, and went into the woods with his axe. When he had gone, several of the monkeys from another part of the forest came at the bidding of Noichi's friends, and scampered into the hut. With their thin yet powerful fingers they parted Noriko's lips, and their claws slipped into the spaces between her teeth. Then, as though they were shelling a stubborn nut, they pulled down her jaw until there was a sharp crack. The sound startled them, and they ran chattering from the hut, but when they gathered the courage to go back, they saw that Noriko's mouth hung open, and they congratulated themselves on their work and returned to their treetop home.

When Noichi came back to the hut for his simple noonday meal, he was overjoyed to find Noriko ready to eat. *Let me hold you up a bit*, he said. *My, but you seem stiff. Some food and drink will do you good. Here now, here…*

With the hachi Noichi fed Noriko several grains of rice at a time, along with a morsel or two of vegetables from the garden. When he poured some water into her mouth, most of it ran back out, but Noichi was still happy that his wife had indicated her willingness to eat by opening her mouth.

There, he said. *Didn't that taste good? You swallow it down when you like. Now rest again.*

Noichi lowered his wife back onto the mat, then ate some rice himself, and went back to work in the forest. When he had gone, several of the sparrows fluttered down and perched upon Noriko's lower lip. They darted their tiny heads inside her sagging mouth and plucked out the grains of rice and bits of greens, flying outside and dropping them while their fellow birds took their places. After a time Noriko's mouth and throat were empty of any trace of food, and it was thus that Noichi discovered her when he came home at the end of the day.

Noichi was pleased that she had decided to swallow the food he had given her, and was certain that she would only continue to improve. He fed her more that evening, telling her what had happened that day as he worked. As he turned his face back to the bowl to spear more grains of rice, the sparrows would dart in to pluck the food from Noriko's mouth so that Noichi found the previous mouthful gone every time. He praised Noriko's appetite and continued to feed her until the bowl was empty. Then he ate and lay down beside her again.

By now darkness had come, and in the light of the dying fire Noichi stroked Noriko's hair and began to kiss her open mouth. *Dear wife*, he said, *if you are too weak or too weary to accept my love, only tell me and I will stop.*

But Noriko made no protestation, so Noichi proceeded with his lovemaking, his tongue entering his wife's cool mouth and stroking her own, lifting it from beneath and feeling it slip away. His hands roved over her body and down to the heart of her womanhood. The dryness which had plagued them before was present, but Noichi applied the salve. When all was ready he lay atop Noriko. Her hips were stiff, undoubtedly, Noichi reasoned, from her long period of inactivity, but with some effort he was able to force her legs apart enough for him to enter her.

The feverishness of his ardor was somewhat cooled by Noriko's seemingly indifferent response, but Noichi persevered, both in the hopes that his own sincere love and desire might yet be matched in intensity by his wife, and from his own simple lust for this woman in his arms, who he had feared would leave him forever. The lust proved more insistent, refusing to wait any longer for the beloved's response, and Noichi broke within his wife with the strength of a gale blowing through the highest trees, snapping the uppermost twigs and branches and hurling them earthward.

For a long moment he lay spent within her, then withdrew and lay on his back beside her, the cool night air drying their sweat-dampened flesh. *Rest now, my dear wife,* he said. *And thank you for your love.*

So the days passed, with Noichi feeding Noriko by day and loving her by night. He grew used to her silences, her lack of response to his affections, and her passivity in all things. In a way he envied it, for she seemed to have reached that state which Noichi had once sought, a complete detachment from the self, no pain, no pleasure, only existence, being in its purest form. At times he felt guilty for forcing upon her such necessities of life as food and propagation (if only attempted), but she could not live without the former nor he without the latter. He also felt ashamed of his weakness of the flesh, but was comforted by the knowledge that Noriko's love for him would selflessly allow such intimacy, even if the act debased the higher state of consciousness which she had attained and to which he as yet could only aspire.

Her meditative focus was such as to make all worldly things unimportant. He fed her, clothed her, and washed her, none of which she would have done on her own. Indeed, her total unconcern with such things was proving a challenge to Noichi. Though he endeavored to see to her cleanliness, it seemed that in her desire to attain pure spirituality she was leaving behind all considerations of the bodily.

The beasts had noticed it long before the smell had reached Noichi's nostrils, and they determined at last that if they were to remain in the presence of their friend whose physical and mental welfare had become paramount to their own, the problem of decay would have to be dealt with immediately, before conditions grew unbearable. Another matter of urgency was that spring was yielding to the warmth of summer, and, although the trees protected the hut from the direct rays of the sun, at the height of summer the small structure grew oppressively hot.

The soft, moist flesh of eyes, tongue, and bowels were those most distressed by putrefaction, and it was these to which the creatures first turned their attention one morning after Noichi's weekly departure for the town of U—. The birds were easily able to dispatch the remnants of the eyes from their deep sockets, raising the drooping lids just far enough for their delicate beaks to pluck away the rotting shards. The tongue was made quick work of by a rat, which buried its head in Noriko's mouth and most efficiently devoured her organ of speech.

In doing so, the rat solved another problem, which was providing further access into the fast mouldering depths of Noriko's corpse. With the tongue gone, the far slimmer weasel was able to slither into Noriko's throat as easily as into its tunnel in the ground. At Noriko's other extremity, where one passage was widened by Noichi's constant nocturnal devotions and the other by the relaxation and atrophy of the surrounding muscles, snakes were able to wend their way into the darkness, scraping away and gathering bits of the suppurating meat in ever-growing balls in their stomachs, being careful not to eat so much that they would become trapped by their own gluttony. Once filled, the snakes would crawl out into the sunshine to digest their meal, at which point others would take their place.

By day's end, dozens of fat-bellied snakes were lying sprawled on rocks in the setting sun, and many full weasels lumbered back to their dens. Most of Noriko's inner organs were gone. Only the tough muscled heart remained, as did the brain in the armored haven of the skull and the tuberous walls of the womb. The creatures were determined, however, that Noichi should find no change in his beloved, and so provided with their own persons what they had removed. Several small otters wormed their way between Noriko's legs and into the now empty cavity of her bowels to provide a fullness there. So that Noichi would not notice the absence of her tongue, a snake which had not as yet fed entered Noriko's empty mouth.

Noichi had ceased feeding Noriko some time earlier, understandably feeling that the depth of his wife's spirituality had made physical food and drink redundant and unnecessary. So upon his return he ate a rice ball and drank some water, all the while chatting to Noriko about the things and the people he had seen in the town and on the road. Then, his simple meal done, Noichi cocked his head and looked at his wife.

You have taken the next step, he said. *The odor of mortality that I have lately detected on you has greatly diminished. Your journey of the spirit proceeds. How proud I am of you! You have attained that state of which I can only dream. Perhaps by your example, wife, your humble husband may someday join you on your upward path. But for now, this poor earthbound soul may only join with you in the manner of a husband and a wife. Please forgive me for my weakness, but through such physical intimacy I may hope to touch your pure spirit as well.*

Then Noichi again visited his caresses upon Noriko, parting her legs and lying upon her and kissing her deeply, and when he placed his tongue between her surrendering lips he was astonished and delighted to find her tongue wrapping around his, as if imbued with a life of its own, and his joy was deep that night.

Every day when Noichi went out to cut wood, the beasts and birds and serpents continued the cleansing of Noriko's body. Within her casing of drying flesh they worked like diligent maids, sweeping out all that was filthy and rotten, leaving behind only what was clean. The snakes, by way of the mouth and nostrils, labored until the skull was free of the decaying brain. The weasels and the rats, like miners in the earth, worked in the fetid darkness until the chest was empty of the slowly decaying heart. The channels of the womb gave way as well to the cleansers' attentions, and was replaced each night by two small rabbits between which lay a soft nest of fur plucked from their generous breasts.

Though the skin was drying nicely in the summer heat, the next few weeks saw the deterioration of the muscles of the breast and arms and legs. The scavengers responded by burrowing into and scouring away the rotting strands, finally loosing into the interior the crayfish and the small crabs, after whose delicate ministrations were finished the corpse was as clean as the Emperor's plates. All that remained of Noriko was dried flesh, hair, bones and what held them together.

The dilemma that now faced Noichi's furred and feathered comrades was that the object of his devotion and desire had become only a woman-shaped leather sack filled with bones. To sustain the illusion, the creatures had to go to astounding lengths every morning, noon and night.

All the animals that were able to do so—the weasels, the badgers, the otters—secreted an oily musk onto Noriko's dried flesh that softened it and gave it the semblance of life. Snakes filled the mouth and cheeks, while weasels and rats and rabbits took their turns inhabiting the cavities of arms and legs, back and chest and neck, buttocks and stomach. Under the flesh of the withered breasts two snakes coiled themselves concentrically so that their heads rested just under the dried teats. And the rabbits flanked the soft nest of the womb.

Noichi accepted the illusion readily, believing because it was his will to believe. He greeted his wife in the morning, visited her at noon, and took her in his arms every night, and if he noticed an odd movement beneath her skin, or heard a soft squeal as he shifted his weight upon her at night, he did not question it, for his wife Noriko was as strange as she was wonderful, and as mysterious as she was miraculous.

One night, holding her in his arms after making love, he said, *If only we could have a child our joy would be complete. I know that it is not possible, yet I did not think it possible that any mortal could achieve the state of being into which you, dear wife, have passed. I will pray that such a thing might occur, and that the love we bear for each other might be perpetuated in a new life made up of our two.*

When the creatures heard Noichi's desire, they were saddened, for their simple minds knew that, although they could create the illusion of life within Noriko's corpse, they could not create new life to spring from within her womb. As it happened, they were not called upon to do so.

One day when Noichi was cutting wood and no creatures were inhabiting the body of Noriko, she gave birth to a Tengu. Several birds and rabbits were there to witness, and they saw the dried skin over Noriko's belly swell and expand. The birds, concerned, drew up Noriko's shift with their beaks so that her lower half was exposed, showing the movement just under the skin. Then Noriko's legs, bony and devoid of muscle, drew apart as though roughly jerked by unseen hands, and the sere lips of her womb parted like the petals of a lotus opening to the sun. Five brownish objects clumped together like a seed pod pressed through the opening and then parted from one another so that the creatures saw they were the fingers of a hand reaching out from within Noriko. A forearm followed, covered, like the hand, with coarse brown hair. The clawed fingers gripped the earth of the floor, creeping along it like a giant spider until another hand appeared, reaching out until it touched the first. Then they parted to either side, pressed into the earth and pulled until a dome of curled hair appeared in the opening through which the arms had come. The matted head pushed itself through, the thick neck bent, and the face looked up at the watching creatures.

A glance from its yellow eyes told them that it was a Tengu, a demon born from Noriko's dead womb, and the birds flew away, and the animals ran into the safety of the forest. So it was that they did not see the rest of the Tengu birth itself from its mother, its shoulders, then trunk, then hips, then legs, then feet come bursting out into the light. Not a trace of fluid from a birth sack shone upon it, for the short, tightly curled brown hair that covered its child-sized body and face was dry. Yet when the last of it had expelled itself from its mother, the opening through which it had passed closed up as tightly as a blossom at midnight.

The first act the Tengu performed after its entry into the world was to kneel and sniff at Noriko's corpse, but finding only dried flesh and no succulent meat there, it covered the corpse with a blanket. Then it crossed its bandy legs and sat on the floor of the hut, waiting for its father.

Noichi returned at nightfall and found the Tengu sitting there. He was surprised and started to back away, but the Tengu sat calmly and spoke to him. *Hello, Father. May I help you stack the wood you have cut today?*

Noichi was confused and asked the Tengu why it called him Father.

Because my mother gave birth to me today. She knew you wanted a child, and she made it come to pass. The Tengu gestured with a clawed hand at the corpse, hidden fully by the blanket. *Mother said that she needs to rest for many days, that birthing me was hard, and that she must regain her former strength through sleep and deep meditation.*

Noichi looked at the Tengu, then at the covered body of his wife, and after a long time he nodded. *My son, your mother has granted me a blessing I thought I would never have. Please accept your father's love. And as a further sign of your mother's power, you are able to speak and walk and reason, all on the day of your birth. Because of this I will call you Shunta* (meaning "Bright Gift").

I do not wish to disagree with you, Father, said the Tengu, *but my mother has already named me Shinta* (meaning "Bringer of Truth").

Then that is what I shall call you, Noichi said, *for your mother's wisdom is great and her attainment to be respected. Now, shall we eat? I have rice and vegetables for your first meal.*

But the Tengu smiled and shook its head. *Like my mother, I have no need of earthly sustenance. My spirit is fed, like hers, by meditation.*

So the Tengu watched Noichi eat, and after Noichi lay on his mat and went to sleep, it went out into the night and hunted, making itself invisible to its prey. At the stream it lay on its belly, blending into the earth, and waited until the otters came out to swim in the moonlight. When an otter and its mate appeared, the Tengu grasped them, one in each hand, snapped both of their necks, and devoured them, eating all, fur, skin, flesh and bones. Then it went behind the hut, dug a large pit with its claws, leaned over it, and retched up the bones, clean and white, so that they fell into the pit.

Then the Tengu went into the part of the forest where the monkeys lived, climbed up into the trees where they slept, and plucked several like fruit, devouring them in the same way as it had the otters, and spewed their bones into the pit. That same night it feasted as well on rabbits, foxes, rats, and a badger, adding their bones to the pile in the pit.

The next morning Noichi awoke to find the Tengu sitting where it had sat the night before. It watched while Noichi ate his breakfast and then went with him into the forest. Noichi cut the wood, and the Tengu carried it back to the hut. But every time the Tengu went to the hut it killed and devoured the creatures that had cared for Noichi.

It crawled up into trees and picked sparrows from the branches, popping them into its mouth and swallowing them after only one crunch of its strong jaws. It did the same with a nest of young rabbits, saving the nursing mother for last. When the Tengu visited the bone pit to bring up the bones, a rat was sniffing about curiously, and the Tengu quickly added it to its breakfast.

Four times it carried back wood that day, and on every trip it devoured more and more of Noichi's friends, and the pile of bones in the pit increased greatly. For several days it did this, until the forest was silent of birdsong, and no creatures sat in the corners of Noichi's hut while he slept. At night the Tengu had to roam further afield, higher up into the hills and further down toward the towns. There were some nights when he barely returned in time to purge the bones from his huge stomach and sit in the hut before Noichi awoke.

There is almost no greater joy for a Tengu than the slow torment of a man, and for this Tengu the sorrow of Noichi over the absence of his friends who had formerly flown, crawled, and scampered all about his hut tasted even better than the flesh and blood of those very creatures he had eaten. The Tengu relished every sorrowful look on Noichi's face when he failed to descry the forms of the foxes waiting for his return from a day of work, or the finches flitting through the air to welcome him home, or the soft and gentle rabbits arching their backs in expectation of his fond petting.

Where have all my friends gone? Noichi asked sadly one night, picking disconsolately at his rice.

The Tengu answered, *Are my mother and I not enough company for you?*

You are fine company, Noichi said. *You are a good son, and a great help in my work. But your mother's meditation remains so deeply focused that I no longer feel a part of her life.*

That will change soon, said the Tengu, with a sly little lick of its lips. *I feel that soon you and my mother will be closer than ever before.*

For a Tengu, the only pleasure greater than the torment of a human is the taste of human flesh, and that taste becomes all the sweeter when the Tengu has first fed upon the tortures of its victim's soul. There was but one physical feast the Tengu would enjoy first.

That night while Noichi slept, the Tengu went outside, took Noichi's axe from the splitting block, and walked over to where the sleeping horse lay. Raising the axe over its head, the Tengu brought down the blade and clove the poor beast's skull in twain so that the brave and strong animal died without a sound. Then the Tengu fed on the horse, starting with its head and sucking it into its maw, which grew wider and wider to accommodate its meal. Then the Tengu proceeded, with great thrusts of its head and the ever wider expansion of its mouth and throat, to swallow the horse's shoulders, like a snake swallowing an egg. The poor beast's forelegs were pressed against its sides as the Tengu continued its meal, and as the demon chewed and swallowed, gouts of blood streamed from its mouth onto the earth. It seemed a reverse birth, with the forest as the womb and the Tengu's ever expanding belly a new dark world into which the horse was being born.

When the Tengu reached the horse's midsection, a snap of its mighty jaws burst the animal's hide like an overcooked dumpling, and blood and bowels spewed out in a flood. But the Tengu continued to chew and swallow, and the loops of bowel were sucked into its maw like strands of soba. The haunches of the horse vanished, and then his rear legs and finally the hooves, and the Tengu was finished with its meal.

As it lumbered toward the bone pit, naked except for its coarse fur, the demon was a grotesque sight. Its child's legs could barely support the huge ball of the stomach, atop which sat the head, its mouth and jaws still as stretched as when it had swallowed the widest part of the horse. When it reached the pit it let itself fall forward onto its great stomach, its gaping mouth over the pit. For a moment, arms and legs in the air, it rocked like an overturned turtle, and then from its maw the Tengu brought up the bones of the horse, white, separated, yet unbroken, and they fell rattling into the pit. Last came the skull, which landed atop the others then rolled down the side.

The girth of the Tengu had been greatly reduced by this purgation, and it pushed itself onto its bandy legs and took a few steps. Then it stopped, shook its still capacious belly back and forth, and heard a dull clattering sound. It turned back to the pit and with something approaching delicacy spat into it four iron horseshoes, one of which twirled around the horse's backbone several times before coming to rest.

Then the Tengu retraced its steps to where it had killed and eaten the horse. There the ground was sodden with blood. It fell upon its knees and licked the earth, its wide tongue sweeping it like a broom until every drop was sucked up. Then it sat in the darkness and let its meal digest. Slowly its stomach and its maw grew smaller until by dawn it had once more attained its original child-like size. It then put the axe back in the splitting block, went into the hut, sat cross-legged, and waited for Noichi to wake.

The light of dawn opened Noichi's eyes, and he smiled wanly at the Tengu he thought his son. He ate his simple breakfast while telling the Tengu of a nightmare he had had (the dream is not recorded), and then went outside. The horse was not standing in its usual place, feeding on the grass that grew around the hut, and this puzzled Noichi. He asked the Tengu, which had followed him in order to watch and relish his discomfiture, if he knew where the horse might be. The Tengu told him that he had strongly sensed that the horse was unhappy with its lot, and that it might have left in the night of its own accord. When Noichi expressed disbelief at this, the Tengu suggested another possibility.

The horse, the Tengu said, *might have been slain and devoured by a Tengu, one of the mountain demons that are said to inhabit these hills. I hear that they can gobble up an animal as large as a horse and then spit out the bones whole. Perhaps that is what occurred. They joy in tormenting men, so perhaps a Tengu knew of your love for the horse, and sought to torture you by destroying it.*

But Noichi replied that he had never seen a Tengu in these parts, and that he could not imagine that even such a creature could be so cruel. The horse must have wandered off and he would search for it. He looked around the hut, the Tengu following him, and his explorations eventually took him to the pit which the Tengu had dug and then filled with the bones of its victims. Noichi stopped and looked into the pit in ever mounting horror. *What is this?* he asked. *Are these bones, so white and dry?*

The Tengu smiled, showing all its long yellow teeth, and gestured proudly toward the pit. *No, Father, not bones but wood. These are the branches and limbs and twigs of white birches that I have cut in the night to surprise you and make you proud of your son. You can sell these in the town of U—for a great deal of money, for white birch is highly prized for its slow burning and its sweet aroma.*

Noichi pointed at several of the larger skulls, including that of the horse. *And what are those, that look so like the skulls of beasts?*

Why, they are knots, Father, said the Tengu. *Knots of wood too tough for my axe to split. I am, after all, only a weak little boy. But I will grow stronger, Father, and my pile of wood will grow ever higher.*

Noichi nodded, then pointed to the horseshoe around the spine of the horse. *And what is that?* he asked, his voice quavering.

An amulet, Father, that some priest may have hung on a tree. A sign of good luck, I am certain. I found three more of them as well.

Noichi nodded, deep in thought. Then he smiled. *I could have no better son,* he said. *You are a fine woodcutter, and you have indeed made me proud. The horse will return to us, and soon your mother will return as well from her inner journey, and good fortune will continue to smile upon us.*

With these words the Tengu knew that Noichi was beyond torment, accepting all the transparent lies and ignoring all the thinly disguised truths with which the demon had been goading him. So the Tengu determined to devour Noichi alive that very night, and decided to start with his feet so that it might hear Noichi's screams as every part of him was slowly swallowed. There is no meat sweeter to a Tengu than man, so as they worked together that day the Tengu's black heart was filled with delighted anticipation, like a gourmand before a meticulously planned banquet. When the sky finally darkened and they headed back to the cottage, the Tengu nearly skipped along with its burden of firewood.

You seem very happy today, my son, Noichi said.

My joy is for you, Father, because I know that you will soon be reunited with Mother.

This remark lightened Noichi's step as well, and it was with glad hearts that both the man and the demon entered the hut. The Tengu sat in the corner and watched while Noichi ate his rice and vegetables and drank his tea. Then Noichi sat by the fire and sharpened the blade of his axe with a stone and water. When he was satisfied he laid the axe on the table, bade a good night to the Tengu, and lay down to sleep on his mat.

The Tengu sat and watched Noichi in the firelight. It was in no hurry, and it savored in its imagination what it would soon taste in truth. But at last it got on its hands and knees and slowly crawled toward Noichi, its gaze fixed on his bare feet. It put its nostrils right next to the man's right foot and sniffed deeply, and was aroused to blood lust by the scent of man flesh. The Tengu opened its mouth, and its jaw dropped onto its chest as its maw expanded to suck in Noichi's foot.

But before it could fasten itself upon and raven the sleeper, a deafening shriek filled the hut, startling the Tengu and jerking Noichi into wakefulness. Both man and demon saw a white form glowing in the yellow firelight, hovering above the earthen floor. It was the ghost of Noriko, and the spirit bore the same fleshly habiliments as its corpse, which still lay on the sleeping mat. Its eye sockets were empty, its cheeks sunken, its skin as dry as parchment, and its long black hair as lank and dead as seaweed washed up onto the rocks. It wore its tired white shift over a body that seemed naught but bones.

Yet it moved with the speed of a moonbeam, and its bony hands fell upon the axe on the table, lifted the blade over its head and brought it down upon the skull of the horrorstruck Tengu. The axe split the demon's head, shearing through bone, but instead of exposing brains, a thick black cloud of darkness drifted from out of the Tengu's shattered skull and vanished like shreds of fog in a strong breeze. The body of the demon collapsed onto the floor, and before Noichi's amazed eyes sank into the earth so that not a hair remained.

Noichi looked back up in terror at the strange apparition that had slain the Tengu, and finally he was able to speak, albeit haltingly and with great fear. *Who…what are you?* he asked.

Noriko's spirit looked at him with no eyes, and the axe fell from her hand onto the floor. *Do you not know me, husband? Do you not know your own dear wife?*

…Noriko? Noichi could scarcely breathe.

The ghost spoke again. *You are a fool, husband. A blind fool. You have been lying with a corpse for many months, imprisoning my spirit within my rotting body by the strength of your love and your madness. Love and madness have made you blind, husband. Every time you thrust into my corpse you tore at my spirit the same way that the wicked samurai captain tore at my flesh. But because I loved you and I knew how much you needed me, my spirit remained silent, praying to the gods that you would eventually realize the truth.*

But your will for illusion was too great, the ghost went on, *so I took your seed into my spirit and from my dead flesh I birthed a Tengu, allowing it a gateway into this world, thinking that once you saw such a hideous creature spawned from the union of the living and the dead that you would surely see the truth. But the Tengu was too clever and you were too blind, accepting all its lies as truth, just the way you accepted the dead as the living. Still, I would have been content to dwell in my hollow corpse for as long as it gave you pleasure, but the Tengu had marked you for death, and my returning was the only way to save the life of my poor, foolish love.*

A smile curled the dry, leathern lips of Noriko's ghost. *I have no eyes,* she went on, *but you are blind. I am dead, husband. Know that. See that. Bury me and leave me at peace. Then cut your wood and live your life, and find love again if you can.*

With these words, the ghost seemed to pour back into her withered corpse under the blanket, and Noichi saw her no more. For a long time the woodcutter lay on his mat, trying to understand what he had seen and heard. He crawled to where the Tengu had disappeared and found no trace of it. Then he crawled to the figure lying under the blanket in the corner. He could make out the shape of the corpse in the flickering firelight, and with a trembling hand he grasped the edge of the blanket and pulled it back.

Noichi gazed upon what lay there until dawn lit the sky. Then he went outside and found a flat rock. With it he dug a hole behind the hut, near the pit in which lay the bones of the Tengu's many victims. When it was deep enough he went back into the hut, wrapped the body of Noriko in the blanket, and took it outside, laying it gently in the grave he had dug. Then he put his mouth close to the corpse's ear and spoke.

My wife, use the great powers of your spirit to sustain your life, for I fear that if I do not do as the demon that visited me last night bade me, she will haunt us again, and it was a terrible demon, for she stole away our son. Perhaps if I sell enough wood I may be able to earn enough money to buy him back from her, and pay a priest to exorcise her so that she will not torment our happy home again.

Then Noichi filled in the grave, weeping for fear that his wife's deep faith would not be enough to preserve her life under the earth. But when he thought of the miraculous things that she had already achieved, his confidence grew, and his tears dried up.

He started to load the cart, and by mid-morning he had filled it so full that he could barely lift it. He no longer had a horse to pull it, for his friend had not returned. So he attached the harness to his own shoulders, cutting it to shorten it and tightening it to fit, and if he leaned forward and trod ahead with all his might, the heavily laden cart followed him. So he began the long journey to the town of U—.

At length he reached the southern road which descended into U—, and quickly found that he could not go first, as the weight of the cart would force him to run faster and faster and would eventually crush him when he could run no more. So he turned the cart and himself about and refit the harness so that he now acted as a brake from behind, digging in his heels and easing the cart down the incline of the road.

The pain in his legs and his back was excruciating, and often the cart would jounce over rocks and into holes so that pieces of Noichi's precious cargo would fall from the cart. Then Noichi would have to stop, put rocks under the wheels, disengage himself from the harness, and retrieve what had fallen, stacking it back on the cart, harnessing himself once more, removing the rocks, and starting again. His progress was sluggish, and not until long after dark did he reach the town of U—. There he dropped exhausted to the ground, crawled under the shelter of his cart, and fell into a deep and dreamless sleep.

In the morning he got to his feet, every limb aching, and pulled his cart into the market square to sell his wares. He was surprised to find the other merchants and the buyers looking at him oddly. Some laughed while others looked disgusted, frowning and turning up their noses. Finally a priest came up to him. *What have you for sale, my friend?* the priest asked.

Noichi smiled. *I have, kind friend, the finest white birch to come from the hills, highly prized for its slow burning and its sweet aroma. It was cut by the hands of my own dear son, Shinta, Bringer of Truth.*

The priest looked at him with pity. *Are you blind, my friend? What you have here is a cart full of bones, nothing more.*

No, no, said Noichi. *You are mistaken. The wood is so white, indeed as white as bone, that it deceives you.*

The priest lifted the horse's skull from the pile. *And what is this?* he asked.

A knot so great as to defy cutting. But it will burn all the same, long and hot.

And the priest, knowing that he was speaking to a madman, put back the skull and walked away.

Noichi stayed in the market square all day long, but no one bought from him. As night approached he shouted to passersby that he must sell his wood, that he must take food home to his wife and his son. When those he accosted told him that he had nothing in his cart but bones, he shouted that they were blinded by illusion.

When darkness came, the priest, who had been thinking of Noichi with pity all day, returned and tried to reason with the woodcutter, urging him to come to the temple and sleep there. *I cannot leave until I have sold my wood*, Noichi said.

And the priest repeated, *I tell you again, my friend, this is not wood but bones.*

And I tell you that that is illusion, Noichi said, and he took from his clothing his flint and steel, and struck them together, and at the very first spark the bones ignited, for they had lain in the sulfurous stomach of the Tengu. The entire cart erupted into white flame, driving the priest back from its searing blaze. But Noichi was too close, and the white heat enveloped him.

The fire burned silently, without a crackle or a hiss, and the priest watched in horror as Noichi stood bathed in white fire, his hair crisped to powder, his flesh sloughing off in blazing sheets, his eyes wide, and his open mouth spewing flame and a single word that filled the priest's ears:

Illusion. Illusion.

By the time men came with water the fire had burned out. Nothing but white ashes was left of the cart and the bones, and where Noichi had stood there remained, cradled in the ashes, only his eyes, miraculously untouched by the fire. The priest took them to the temple where they are to this day, undefiled by decay or by the years, encased in a reliquary that bears the legend:

THE EYES OF NOICHI THE BLIND
WHO IN LIFE AND DEATH
SPOKE THE TRUTH OF THE BUDDHA:
ALL IS ILLUSION.

Afterword

by Alan Drew, PhD.

University of Western Michigan

When Chet Williamson first contacted me regarding "The Story of Noichi the Blind," I was intrigued if pessimistic. Lafcadio Hearn's writings have been assiduously compiled and studied by a host of scholars and aficionados since his death, and the prospect of a previously unknown story from his hand surfacing after a century was highly unlikely. Still, it was possible, and I agreed to look at the manuscript and share my opinion as to the authorship of the work.

I read it first as pure story, in order to form an initial impression before delving into it textually, and readily agreed with Mr. Williamson regarding the unlikelihood of its publication during Hearn's lifetime, due to its extremely outspoken sexual content. The horrific elements were, as well, perhaps too explicitly stated for the tastes of Hearn's contemporaries.

The tale contains many parallels to Hearn's known stories, some quite obvious, others more subtle. In terms of theme and plot, the storyline of a wife or a mistress's ghost returning to correct or take vengeance upon her husband or lover was frequently used by Hearn.

"The Story of O-Kamè" from Hearn's collection, *Kottō*, relates the tale of a wife returning nightly to her husband's side to vampirically draw away his strength; "A Passional Karma" from *In Ghostly Japan* tells of the samurai Shinzaburō, haunted unto a grisly death by the ghost of the spurned O-Tsuyu; and "The Reconciliation" from *Shadowings* tells the story of still another unfaithful samurai who returns to his deserted wife after several years, finds her alive and unchanged, and wakes up the following morning beside her desiccated corpse.

Certain elements of the Tengu, a mountain demon, may also be found in Hearn's stories, although the agreeable avian creature depicted in "Story of a Tengu" (*In Ghostly Japan*) has little in common with the flesh-eating monster of "The Story of Noichi the Blind." This violent and duplicitous Tengu hearkens back to the earlier, pre-14th century depictions of the demon as a purely evil being, rather than the beneficial Tengu of the 18th and 19th centuries that were honored as mountain deities.

The dietary habits of this unknown author's Tengu are similar to that of the man-eating goblin which is the title character of Hearn's "Jikininki" (*Kwaidan*), and which devours a corpse "more quickly than a cat devours a rat—beginning at the head, and eating everything: the hair and the bones and even the shroud." Eating of the dead may also be found in section VI of "Of Ghosts and Goblins" in Hearn's *Glimpses of Unfamiliar Japan*. In a harrowing scene, a young woman takes her suitor to a cemetery at midnight, where she rifles a grave and begins to devour what appears to be the arm of a child, passing part of it to the samurai and telling him to do the same. He does, and so finds the arm made of *kwashi*, a Japanese confection. The woman was merely testing the courage of her suitor, who she then weds. There is no such happy ending to "The Story of Noichi the Blind."

The theme of necrophilia, which is treated so overtly in this newly found story, is more problematic when discussing the parallels with Hearn's stories. "The Corpse-Rider" from *Shadowings* is the closest Hearn ever came to the forbidden subject. In this very brief folk tale, a divorced husband is instructed by an inyôshi (a spiritual master) to sit on the back of his dead ex-wife and hold her hair through the night if he is to avoid being killed by her vengeful spirit. He does so, and rides her through the darkness, the wife "always bearing the weight of the man" as he hears the continual "hiss of her breathing." When the ride is finished: "Under the man she panted and moaned till the cocks began to crow. Thereafter she lay still." This is a far cry from the straightforward sexual intercourse in which Noichi engages with the corpse of Noriko, but the explicit depiction of a man riding a corpse provides a suitable segue into Hearn's use of graphic horror.

Scholars have long heralded Lafcadio Hearn's delicacy and subtlety even when describing the most dreadful horrors, but there are many examples of Hearn engaging in vivid pictorial descriptions that would challenge even the most bloodthirsty of today's film directors to adequately depict on the screen. "Of a Promise Broken" (*A Japanese Miscellany*) ends with the *grand guignol* image of the animated corpse of a first wife holding the head of the second, which she has ripped off the woman's body. "But the fleshless right hand, though parted from the wrist, still writhed;—and its fingers still gripped at the bleeding head—and tore, and mangled—as the claws of a yellow crab cling fast to a fallen fruit..."

A similar image is found in "Ingwa-banashi" (*In Ghostly Japan*), though a highly-charged sexual element is added to this story of another first wife avenging herself on her successor. The dying woman asks to be carried on the girl's back, and then slips her hands down the front of the girl's robe to clutch her breasts, and dies. The hands, which "appeared to have grown into the quick flesh," cannot be removed, and have to be cut off at the wrists. They soon dry up but every night at the Hour of the Ox, "they would stir—stealthily, like great grey spiders...they would clutch and compress and torture" the victim.

Hearn supplies other moments of graphic terror in many stories, such as the previously mentioned "A Passional Karma," in which a servant spies on his master and his ghostly paramour: "For the face was the face of a woman long dead,—and the fingers caressing were fingers of naked bone." The tale's climax is neither delicate nor subtle: "Shinzaburō was dead—hideously dead;—and his face was the face of a man who had died in the uttermost agony of fear;—and lying beside him in the bed were the bones of a woman! And the bones of the arms, and the bones of the hands, clung fast about his neck." The similar horrors of

"The Story of Noichi the Blind" are not all that dissimilar to these "shilling shocker" climaxes of Hearn's.

One final parallel worth mentioning is the symbolic use of the axe in "The Story of Noichi the Blind" and in a tale of Hearn's from *Kottō*, "The Eater of Dreams." The axe is Noichi's only tool, the utilitarian object by which he makes his meager living, and also the object with which Noriko's ghost kills the threatening Tengu and saves her husband's life. Through this act, she is finally able to explain to him the truth, which he then rejects for his own truth, which is ironically interpreted by the priest as the teaching of the Buddha. In Hearn's "The Eater of Dreams," the narrator destroys his dream-self with an axe, at which point the dream-eating Baku says, "The axe—yes! the Axe of the Excellent Law, by which the monster of Self is utterly destroyed!...The best kind of a dream! My friends, *I* believe in the teachings of the Buddha." In both stories, the axe is the freeing element of both destruction and creation—the destruction of the dark Self, and the creation of the knowledge of the path of Buddha.

Still, all these parallels between "The Story of Noichi the Blind" and Hearn's own works take not one step toward proving that Hearn was the author of this newly discovered story. In fact, the evidence against it being an undiscovered Hearn tale is too great to even suggest that possibility. I should now like to offer several tangible arguments against Hearn's authorship:

The first and strongest piece of evidence is the fact that the manuscript is typewritten. Hearn unfailingly wrote in longhand, and the eyesight in his one good eye was so bad that his face had to be several inches from the paper, making typing difficult if not impossible. It is quite unlikely that the story would have been dictated by Hearn to a typist, and equally doubtful that it was transcribed from one of Hearn's handwritten manuscripts.

Nearly all of Hearn's Japanese stories were retellings of folk tales recorded in earlier volumes. Hearn is quite clear about crediting those volumes, naming them specifically. The plot of "The Story of Noichi the Blind" has no parallel in any of the volumes Hearn used, or in any others that I have read.

There are also numerous errors in period detail. The description of the samurai's horse which Noichi befriends provides three obvious examples: samurai horsemen did not wear spurs, reins were made not of leather but of silk or cotton cord, and horses were not shod. The scene with the Tengu spitting up the horseshoes and getting a "ringer" is only one instance in which the writer sacrifices authenticity for a twisted joke.

Looking at purely textual evidence, Hearn unfailingly used quotation marks for the dialogue in his Japanese stories, while the "Noichi" author underlined the words of dialogue in the typescript to indicate italics.

Hearn's punctuation was at times eccentric, with the use of colons, semi-colons, and commas preceding an em dash (as in the quotations above). Nothing of the sort is found in the "Noichi" manuscript.

Hearn was meticulous concerning the use of diacritical marks. In his "The Story of Mimi-Nashi-Hōïchi," the name Hōïchi always has the proper marks. The name "Noichi" has no such marks typed or handwritten in. Also, "Noichi" is very uncommon as a proper name, particularly in the era in which the story seems to be set.

In fact, the very name "Noichi the Blind" seems a literary *homage* to "Hōïchi the Earless," the protagonist of the above-mentioned story. It is hardly an honor that Hearn would have paid to himself.

Finally, moving from the concrete to the intangible and the arena of "gut feeling," the story itself, from a literary rather than textual viewpoint, reads to me less like Lafcadio Hearn than like someone trying to write in his style. The attempt is more flattering than successful. Hearn's prose was far more effortless and far less self-conscious than the writing here. As for the subject matter, the story is so disturbing in its perverted sexuality that it holds more interest as a study in Freudian authorial pathology than as a literary work. Its sensationalism may nonetheless appeal to some readers, and the trustees of the university at which I teach fortunately shared my opinion that it would be instructive to have the work appear in print to satisfy the curiosity of those Hearn scholars and devotees who might have become aware of its existence, and to put to rest any remaining rumors of Hearn's authorship.

For the final verdict, as Mr. Williamson suggests in his introduction, must be that "The Story of Noichi the Blind" is almost certainly a wrongheaded *homage* to Lafcadio Hearn by an English-speaking writer probably living in Japan, written after Hearn's death, but before 1940.

Unless further evidence is forthcoming, the author of the work will probably never be identified, which may be just as well for his reputation and that of his survivors.

Alan Drew is the author of Lafcadio Hearn: A Spark in the Shadows, *editor of* Lafcadio Hearn and Basil Hall Chamberlain: A Friendship in Letters, *and author of many other books and articles.*

About the Author

Chet Williamson has written mystery and suspense for 40 years. Among his novels are *Second Chance, Hunters, Defenders of the Faith, Ash Wednesday*, and *Psycho: Sanitarium*. His short stories have appeared in *The New Yorker, Playboy, Esquire,* and many other magazines and anthologies. He has won the International Horror Guild Award, and has been shortlisted for the Edgar Award, the World Fantasy Award, and the HWA's Stoker Award. He has recorded over 50 audiobooks, both of his own work and that of many other writers. Follow him on Twitter (@chetwill) or at www.chetwilliamson.com.

Curious about other Crossroad Press books? Stop by our website:
http://crossroadpress.com
We offer quality writing
in digital, audio, and print formats.

Subscribe to our newsletter on the website homepage and receive a free
eBook.

www.ingramcontent.com/pod-product-compliance
Lightning Source LLC
Chambersburg PA
CBHW022054170626
46808CB00003B/1467